P9-CJT-243

Here's what kids and grown-ups have to say about the Magic Tree House® books:

"Oh, man . . . the Magic Tree House series
is really exciting!"
—Christina

"I like the Magic Tree House series. I stay up
all night reading them. Even on school nights!"
—Peter

"Jack and Annie have opened a door to a world
of literacy that I know will continue throughout
the lives of my students."
—Deborah H.

"As a librarian, I have seen many happy young
readers coming into the library to check out
the next Magic Tree House book in the series."
—Lynne H.

Magic Tree House®

For a list of Magic Tree House® Merlin Missions and other Magic Tree House® titles, visit MagicTreeHouse.com.

Osborne, Mary Pope.
Pirates past noon

1994
33305250455965
ca   07/05/22

TREE HOUSE

#4 PIRATES PAST NOON

BY MARY POPE OSBORNE
ILLUSTRATED BY SAL MURDOCCA

A STEPPING STONE BOOK™

Random House 🏠 New York

For Andrew Kim Boyce

This is a work of fiction. Names, characters, places, and incidents either are the product of the author's imagination or are used fictitiously. Any resemblance to actual persons, living or dead, events, or locales is entirely coincidental.

Text copyright © 1994 by Mary Pope Osborne
Cover art and interior illustrations copyright © 1994 by Sal Murdocca

All rights reserved. Published in the United States by Random House Children's Books, a division of Penguin Random House LLC, New York. Originally published in paperback in the United States by Random House Children's Books, New York, in 1994.

Random House and the colophon are registered trademarks and A Stepping Stone Book and the colophon are trademarks of Penguin Random House LLC. Magic Tree House is a registered trademark of Mary Pope Osborne; used under license.

Visit us on the Web!
SteppingStonesBooks.com
randomhousekids.com
MagicTreeHouse.com

Educators and librarians, for a variety of teaching tools, visit us at
RHTeachersLibrarians.com

Library of Congress Cataloging-in-Publication Data
Osborne, Mary Pope.
Pirates past noon / by Mary Pope Osborne ; illustrated by Sal Murdocca.
p. cm.
(The Magic Tree House) A First Stepping Stone book.
Summary: The magic tree house whisks Jack and Annie back to the days of deserted islands, secret maps, hidden gold, and nasty pirates.
ISBN 978-0-679-82425-1 (trade) — ISBN 978-0-679-92425-8 (lib. bdg.) —
ISBN 978-0-375-89421-3 (ebook)
[1. Pirates—Fiction. 2. Time travel—Fiction. 3. Magic—Fiction. 4. Tree houses—Fiction.]
I. Murdocca, Sal, ill. II. Title. III. Series: Osborne, Mary Pope. Magic tree house series ; #4.
PZ7.O81167Pi 1994 [Fic]—dc20 93-2039

Printed in the United States of America

100 99 98 97 96 95 94 93 92

This book has been officially leveled by using the F&P Text Level Gradient™ Leveling System.

Random House Children's Books supports the First Amendment and celebrates the right to read.

Contents

1

Too Late!

Jack stared out his bedroom window. The rain kept falling. And falling.

"The TV said it would stop by noon," said Annie, his seven-year-old sister.

"It's already past noon," said Jack.

"But we have to go to the tree house," said Annie. "I have a feeling the M person will be there today."

Jack pushed his glasses into place and took a deep breath. He wasn't sure he was ready to meet the M person yet. The mysterious person who had put all the books in the magic tree house.

"Come on," said Annie.

Jack sighed. "Okay," he said. "You get our raincoats and boots. I'll get the medallion and bookmark."

Annie ran to get their rain gear.

Jack reached into his drawer. He took out the medallion.

It was gold. The letter M was engraved on it.

Then he took out the bookmark. It was made of blue leather. It had the same M on it.

Both M's matched the M that was on the floor of the tree house.

Jack put the medallion and bookmark into his backpack. Then he threw in his notebook and pencil. Jack liked to take notes about important things.

2

"I got our rain stuff!" called Annie.

Jack picked up his pack and went downstairs. Annie was waiting by the back door. She was putting on her boots. "Meet you outside," she said.

Jack pulled on his raincoat and boots. Then he put on his backpack and joined her.

The wind was blowing hard.

"Ready! Set! Go!" shouted Annie.

They kept their heads down and charged into the rainy wind.

Soon they were in the Frog Creek woods.

Tree branches swayed, flinging rainwater everywhere.

"Yuck!" said Annie.

They splashed through puddles. Until they came to the tallest oak tree in the woods.

They looked up.

Tucked between two branches was the tree house. It looked dark and lonely against the stormy sky.

Hanging from the tree house was a rope ladder. It was blowing in the wind.

Jack thought of all the books up there. He hoped they weren't getting wet.

"The M person's been there," said Annie.

Jack caught his breath. "How can you tell?" he said.

"I can feel it," she whispered.

She grabbed the rope ladder and started up. Jack followed.

Inside the tree house it was chilly and damp.

But the books were dry. They were all neatly stacked along the wall. Just the way they had been the day before.

Annie picked up a castle book on top of

one stack. It had taken them to the time of castles.

"Remember the knight?" she said.

Jack nodded. He would never forget the knight who had helped them.

Annie put down the castle book. She picked up the next book on the stack.

It was the dinosaur book that had taken them to the time of dinosaurs.

"Remember?" she said.

Jack nodded.

He'd never forget the pteranodon who had saved him from the Tyrannosaurus rex.

Then Annie held up a book about ancient Egypt.

"Meow," she said.

Jack smiled. The Egypt book had taken them to the time of pyramids. A black cat had come to the rescue there.

"And here's the book about home," Annie said.

She held up the book with the picture of their hometown in it.

Frog Creek, Pennsylvania.

Jack smiled again. The Pennsylvania book had brought them back home at the end of each of their adventures.

Jack sighed. Okay. He still had two main questions.

Who was the M person who had put all the books here?

And did the knight, the pteranodon, and the cat all know the M person?

Finally Jack reached into his backpack. He took out the gold medallion and the leather bookmark. He placed them on the floor. Right over the spot where the M glowed faintly in the wood.

Rain blew into the tree house.

"Brr!" said Annie. "It's not very cozy today."

Jack agreed with her. It was too wet and cold.

"Look." Annie pointed to an open book lying in the corner. "I don't remember a book being open."

"Me neither," said Jack.

Annie picked up the book. She stared at the picture on the page.

"Wow, this place looks great." She showed the picture to Jack.

He saw a sunny beach. A big green parrot sitting in a palm tree. And a ship sailing on a blue sea.

Another gust of rainy wind blew into the tree house.

Annie pointed to the picture. "I wish we

were there instead of here," she said.

"Yeah," said Jack. "But where is there?"

"Too late!" came a squawk.

Jack and Annie turned quickly.

Sitting on a branch outside the window ledge of the tree house was a green parrot. Exactly like the parrot in the picture.

"Too late!" the parrot squawked again.

"A talking parrot!" said Annie. "Is your name Polly? Can I call you Polly?"

Suddenly the wind started to whistle.

"Oh no! Now we're in big trouble!" said Jack.

The wind blew harder.

The leaves shook.

The tree house started to spin. Faster and faster!

Jack squeezed his eyes shut. Then everything was still.

Absolutely still.

Jack opened his eyes.

"Too late!" squawked Polly.

2

The Bright Blue Sea

Jack felt hot sunlight streaming into the tree house.

He smelled saltwater.

He heard the sound of waves.

He and Annie looked out the window.

The tree house was in a palm tree. Beyond was a bright blue sea. A tall sailing ship was on the horizon. It was just like the picture in the book.

"Too late!" squawked Polly.

"Look!" said Annie.

Polly was flying in circles above the tree

house. Then she swooped down to the ocean.

"Come on, let's follow her! Let's go in the water!" said Annie. She took off her raincoat and dropped it on the floor.

"Wait, we have to study the book first," said Jack. He started to reach for the book. But Annie grabbed it.

"You can read it on the beach," she said. Without even looking at the cover, she shoved the book into Jack's backpack.

He sighed. Actually, the water *did* look wonderful.

"Okay," Jack said. He took off his raincoat, too.

"Come on!" Annie handed Jack his backpack, then started down the ladder.

Jack folded the raincoat and put it next to the stack of books. He put on his backpack. Then he went down the ladder.

As soon as Annie hit the sand, she ran toward the ocean. Jack watched her wade into the water. She was still wearing her rain boots.

"Your boots, Annie," called Jack.

She shrugged. "They'll dry out," she said.

Jack took off his boots and socks. He put them beside his pack. Then he rolled up his jeans. And ran across the hot sand into the waves.

The water was warm and clear. Jack could see shells and tiny fishes.

He shielded his eyes against the sun. And peered out at the sea.

The tall sailing ship seemed a bit closer.

"Where's Polly?" said Annie.

Jack glanced around. No sign of Polly. Not in the palm trees. Not on the sunlit sand. Not over the bright blue sea.

When Jack looked out at the sea again, the ship seemed even closer. Now Jack could see its flag.

As he stared at the ship's flag, a chill went through him.

The flag was black. *With a skull and crossbones.*

"Oh man," he breathed. He started out of the water.

"What's wrong?" said Annie. She splashed after him.

Jack ran to his backpack. Annie followed.

He grabbed the book from his backpack. He looked at the cover. For the first time, he and Annie read the title of the book.

"Yikes!" said Annie.

"Pirates of the Caribbean," Jack read aloud.

3

Three Men in a Boat

"We've come to the time of pirates!" Jack said.

"Pirates?" squeaked Annie. "Like in *Peter Pan?*"

Jack flipped to the picture that showed the parrot, the sea and the ship.

He read the caption under the picture:

> Three hundred years ago, pirates raided Spanish treasure ships in the Caribbean Sea.

He grabbed his notebook and pencil from his pack. He wrote:

pirates in the Caribbean

He turned to the next page. There was a picture of a pirate flag. He read:

> The skull-and-crossbones flag was
> called the Jolly Roger.

"Let's go!" said Annie.

"Wait!" said Jack. "I want to make a drawing of the flag."

He propped the pirate book in the sand.

He started drawing the Jolly Roger flag.

"Don't copy the picture in the book," said Annie. "Look at the real thing."

But Jack pushed his glasses into place and kept drawing.

"Jack, some pirates are getting into a rowboat," said Annie.

Jack kept drawing.

"Jack, the boat's leaving the big ship," said Annie.

"What?" Jack looked up.

"Look." Annie pointed.

Jack looked. He saw the rowboat coming toward the shore.

"Run!" said Annie. She started running toward the tree house.

Jack jumped up. His glasses fell off.

"Hurry!" Annie called back to him.

Jack went down on his knees. He felt for his glasses. Where were they?

Jack saw something glinting in the sand. He reached for it. It was his glasses. He snatched them up.

Then he threw his notebook and pencil

18

into his pack. He put the pack on his back.

He grabbed his boots and his socks. And he took off running.

"Hurry! They're coming!" Annie was at the top of the rope ladder.

Jack looked back at the sea. The pirates were closer to the shore.

Suddenly Jack saw the pirate book. In all the confusion he had forgotten it. It was still propped in the sand.

"Oh man, I forgot the book!" he said. He dropped his socks and boots below the tree house.

"Come on, Jack!" Annie shouted.

"I'll be right back!" Jack called. "I've got to get the book!"

"Jack, forget it!"

But Jack was already running toward the water.

Jack grabbed the book.

"Come back!" Annie shouted.

Jack shoved the book into his backpack.

Suddenly a giant wave carried the rowboat right onto the beach.

"Run, Jack!" shouted Annie.

Three big pirates splashed onto the sand.

They had knives in their teeth.

They had pistols in their belts.

They charged toward Jack.

"Run, Jack, run!" cried Annie.

4

Vile Booty

Jack started to run across the hot sand. He ran as fast as he could.

But the pirates ran faster.

Before Jack knew it, the biggest pirate had grabbed him!

Jack struggled. But the pirate had huge, strong arms. He held on to Jack and laughed a mean, ugly laugh. He had a shaggy black beard. A patch covered one eye.

Jack heard Annie yelling. He saw her coming down the rope ladder.

"Stay where you are!" Jack shouted.

But Annie kept coming. "Leave him alone, you bully!" she cried.

The other two pirates laughed meanly. They were dirty and ragged.

Annie charged up to the biggest pirate. "Let him go!" she said. She hit the pirate with her fist and kicked him.

But the pirate just growled. Then he grabbed her, too. And with his giant hands, he held Jack and Annie as if they were two kittens.

"*No* one escapes Cap'n Bones!" he roared. His breath was terrible.

"Let go!" Annie shouted into his face.

But Cap'n Bones just smiled. All his teeth were black.

Annie fell silent.

Cap'n Bones laughed loudly. Then he turned to the other two.

"Find out what's in their house, you dogs," he said.

"Aye, aye, Cap'n!" they answered. And they started up the ladder to the tree house.

"What do you spy, Pinky?" shouted Cap'n Bones.

"Books, Cap'n!" Pinky shouted down.

"Aghh, books," growled Cap'n Bones. He spit on the sand. "I want gold, you dogs!"

"Dogs are nicer than you," said Annie.

"Shhh," said Jack.

"What about you, Stinky?" Cap'n Bones roared.

"Just books, Cap'n!" shouted Stinky.

"Aghh, books," said Cap'n Bones. He spit on the sand again. "I hate books! Keep looking, dogs! Find me something good!"

Cap'n Bones grabbed Jack's backpack.

"What's in here?" he said.

"Nothing—" Jack quickly opened the pack. "Just paper, a pencil, a book."

"Another book!" roared Cap'n Bones. "That's vile booty!"

A gleeful shriek pierced the air.

Cap'n Bones froze. "What's that?" he shouted.

"Look, Cap'n! Look!"

Pinky leaned out the tree house window. He held the medallion. It glimmered in the sunlight.

Oh brother, thought Jack.

"Throw it down!" cried Cap'n Bones.

"It's not yours!" shouted Annie.

Cap'n Bones dropped Jack and Annie. He caught the medallion as it fell.

"Gold! Gold! Gold!" he cried. Cap'n Bones

threw back his head and laughed horribly.

He grabbed two of his pistols. He shot them into the air. Pinky and Stinky howled like wolves.

5

The Kid's Treasure

Jack and Annie watched in horror.

The gold-greedy pirates seemed to have lost their minds.

Jack nudged Annie. Together they started to back slowly away from the pirates. Toward the tree house.

"Halt!" Cap'n Bones shouted. He aimed his pistols at them. "Not another step, lubbers!"

Jack and Annie froze.

Cap'n Bones grinned his black-toothed grin. "Tell old Bones where the rest is," he growled. "Or prepare to meet thy doom."

"What—what rest?" said Annie.

"The rest of the treasure!" roared Cap'n Bones. "I know it's on this island. I have a map!"

He reached into a belt pouch and pulled out a torn piece of paper. He waved it at Jack and Annie.

"Is that a treasure map?" asked Jack.

"Aye, it's the map telling about Kidd's treasure."

"Which kid's treasure? Not *us* kids," said Annie. "We don't know anything about a kid's treasure."

"Why don't you read the map?" said Jack.

"*You* read it!" Cap'n Bones shoved the map in Jack's face.

Jack stared at the strange marks on the paper.

"What does that mean?" asked Jack.

"What does *what* mean?" asked Cap'n Bones.

"Those words." Jack pointed at the words at the bottom of the map.

"Well, it means..." Cap'n Bones' good eye squinted at the writing. He frowned. He coughed. He rubbed his nose.

"Aw, leave him alone," Pinky growled at Jack.

"You know he can't read," said Stinky.

"Shut up!" Cap'n Bones roared at his men.

"Jack and I can read," Annie piped up.

"Shhh," said Jack.

"Cap'n, make 'em read the map!" said Stinky.

Cap'n Bones gave Jack and Annie a dark look. "Read it," he growled.

"Then will you let us go?" said Jack.

The gold doth lie beneath the whale's eye.

The pirate squinted his good eye. "Aye, lubber. When the treasure's in me hands, I'll let you go."

"Okay," said Jack. "I'll read it to you." He looked at the map. "It says, *The gold doth lie beneath the whale's eye.*"

"Heh?" Cap'n Bones scowled. "What's that supposed to mean, lubber?"

Jack shrugged.

"Hang it! Take 'em hack to the ship!" shouted Cap'n Bones. "They can rot there till they're ready to tell us how to find Kidd's treasure!"

Jack and Annie were tossed into the rowboat.

Waves splashed the sides. The sky ahead was dark with thunderclouds. A strong wind had started to blow.

"Row, dogs, row!" said Cap'n Bones.

Pinky and Stinky began rowing toward the big ship.

"Look!" Annie said to Jack. She pointed to the shore.

Polly the parrot was flying over the sand.

"She wants to help us," whispered Annie.

Polly started to fly out over the waves. But the winds were too strong. She turned around and flew back to the island.

6

The Whale's Eye

The rowboat tossed from side to side. The waves were huge. Salty spray stung Jack's eyes. He felt seasick.

"Hold 'er steady!" shouted Cap'n Bones.

He pointed at the sea. "Or we'll be meat for those evil brutes!"

Dark fins cut through the water. *Sharks.* One zoomed right by the boat. Jack could have reached out and touched it.

He shuddered.

Soon the rowboat pulled alongside the ship.

The air was filled with wild fiddle music and bagpipes playing. And Jack heard jeers, shouts, and ugly laughter.

"Hoist 'em aboard!" Cap'n Bones shouted to his men.

Annie and Jack were hauled onto the deck. The ship creaked and moaned. It rolled from side to side. Ropes flapped and snapped in the wild wind.

Everywhere they looked, Jack and Annie saw pirates.

Some were dancing. Some were drinking. Many were fighting. With swords. Or with their fists.

"Lock 'em in my cabin!" Cap'n Bones ordered.

A couple of pirates grabbed Jack and Annie. And threw them in the ship's cabin. Then locked the door.

The air inside the cabin was damp and sour-smelling. A shaft of gray light came through a small round window.

"Oh man," said Jack. "We've got to figure out how to get back to the island."

"So we can get into the tree house and go home," said Annie.

"Right." Jack suddenly felt tired. How would they ever get out of this mess?

"We better examine the book," he said.

He reached into his pack and pulled out the pirate book.

He flipped through the pages.

He looked for information to help them.

"Look," he said.

He found a picture of pirates burying a treasure chest. "This might help."

Together they read the words under the picture.

> Captain Kidd was a famous pirate. It is said that he buried a treasure chest on a deserted island. The chest was filled with gold and jewels.

"Captain Kidd!" said Jack.

"So *that's* the *kid* that Bones keeps talking about," said Annie.

"Right," said Jack.

Annie looked out the round window.

"And Captain Kidd's treasure is buried somewhere on the island," she said.

Jack took out his notebook and pencil. He wrote:

Captain Kidd's treasure
on island

"Ja-ack," Annie said.

"Shhh, wait a minute," he said. "I'm thinking."

"Guess what I see?" said Annie.

"What?" Jack asked. He looked back at the book.

"A whale."

"Neat," he said. Then he looked up. "A whale? Did you say . . . a whale?"

"A whale. A huge whale. As big as a football field."

Jack jumped up and looked out the window with her.

"Where?" Jack asked. All he could see was the island. And stormy waves. And shark fins.

"There!" said Annie.

"Where? Where?"

"There! The *island* is shaped like a giant whale!"

"Oh man," whispered Jack. Now he could see it.

"See the whale's back?" said Annie.

"Yep." The slope of the island looked like the back of a whale.

"See his spout?" said Annie.

"Yep." The palm tree that held the tree house looked like the spout of the whale.

"See his eye?" said Annie.

"Yep." A big black rock looked like the eye of the whale.

"The gold doth lie beneath the whale's eye," whispered Jack. "Wow."

7

Gale's a-Blowin'

"So the treasure must be under that rock," said Annie.

"Right," said Jack. "Now we just have to get back to the island. We'll show Cap'n Bones where the treasure is. Then while all the pirates are digging, we'll sneak up to the tree house."

"And make a wish to go home," said Annie.

"Right." Jack poked his head out of the round window of the cabin. "Cap'n Bones, sir!" he shouted.

The pirates took up the cry. "Cap'n Bones! Cap'n Bones!"

"Hey?" came a horrible voice.

Cap'n Bones stuck his ugly face through the window. His good eye glared at Jack. "What do you want, lubbers?"

"We're ready to tell the truth, sir," said Jack.

"Go ahead," growled Cap'n Bones.

"We know where Captain Kidd's treasure is."

"Where?"

"We can't just tell you. We have to *show* you," said Annie.

Cap'n Bones gave Annie and Jack a long hard look.

"You'll need a rope," said Jack.

"And shovels," said Annie.

Cap'n Bones growled. Then he roared at

his men, "Get some rope and shovels!"

"Aye, aye, Cap'n!"

"Then throw these lubbers in the boat! We're going back to the island!"

"Aye, aye, Cap'n!"

Back in the rowboat, Jack saw the sky had grown even darker with clouds. The waves were bigger. The wind was howling.

"Gale's a-blowin'!" said Pinky.

"You'll see a gale if I don't get me gold today, by thunder!" Cap'n Bones shouted. "Row, dogs, row!"

The three pirates battled the waves, until the rowboat reached the island. They all piled onto the shore.

Cap'n Bones grabbed Jack and Annie.

"Okay, lubbers," he said. "Now show us where the treasure is."

"There," said Annie. She pointed at the

black rock near the tip of the island.

"Under that rock," said Jack.

Cap'n Bones dragged Jack and Annie down the beach to the black rock.

"Get to work!" Cap'n Bones said to Pinky and Stinky.

"What about you?" said Annie.

"Me? Work?" Cap'n Bones chuckled.

Jack gulped. How could they get away from him?

"Don't you think you should help your friends?" he said.

Cap'n Bones gave Jack a horrible grin. "Nay. I'm going to hold you two—till there's treasure in me hands!"

8

Dig, Dogs, Dig

Pinky and Stinky tied their rope around the big rock.

The wind howled. The two pirates pulled. And pulled. And pulled.

"They need help!" said Jack.

"Aghh, let the dogs do the work!" growled Cap'n Bones.

"You're not very nice to them," said Annie.

"Who cares?" roared Cap'n Bones.

"Cap'n! We got it!" shouted Pinky.

They started pulling the rock across the sand.

"Now let's dig where the rock was," said Jack. "All of us!"

But Cap'n Bones ignored his suggestion.

"Dig, you dogs!" he shouted.

Pinky and Stinky started to dig. The wind blew even harder. There was going to be a thunderstorm.

"Oww! I got sand in me eyes!" Pinky whined.

"Oww! Me back hurts!" Stinky cried.

"Dig!" shouted Cap'n Bones. He held Jack and Annie with one hand. With the other he pulled out the gold medallion.

He tossed it at the two pirates. It fell into the hole.

"Dig for more of these, you swine!" he said.

Squawk!

"Look!" Annie said.

Polly was back! She was circling above them!

"Go back!" she squawked.

47

Stinky and Pinky looked up at the parrot. They scowled.

"Dig!" shouted Cap'n Bones.

"A big storm is comin', Cap'n!" said Pinky.

"Go back!" said Polly.

"The bird's an omen, Cap'n!" shouted Stinky.

"Dig, you dogs!" cried Cap'n Bones.

"Go back!" squawked Polly.

"The bird's warning us!" shouted Pinky. "We've got to get to the ship before it's too late!"

The two pirates threw down their shovels. They started running toward the rowboat.

"Mutineers! Come back!" shouted Cap'n Bones. He dragged Jack and Annie down the beach as he ran after his men. "Stop!"

But the pirates kept running. They got to the rowboat and pushed it into the sea.

"Wait!" cried Cap'n Bones.

Pinky and Stinky jumped into the boat. They started rowing.

"Wait!" Cap'n Bones let go of Jack and Annie. He ran into the water. "Wait, you dogs!"

He hauled himself into the rowboat.

Then the three pirates disappeared into the spray of the waves.

"Go back!" squawked Polly.

"She means *us*!" said Annie.

Just then the storm broke over the island. The wind howled. Rain fell in buckets.

"Let's go!" cried Annie.

"Wait! I have to get the medallion!" shouted Jack. He ran to the hole dug by the pirates. He looked down in it.

Even in the dreary light, the medallion was shining.

Big, fat raindrops were falling into the hole, washing away the sand.

Jack saw a patch of wood.

Then the rain cleared away more sand. And Jack saw the top of an old trunk.

He stared. Was it Captain Kidd's treasure chest?

"Hurry, Jack!" cried Annie. She was half-way up the tree house ladder.

"I found it! I found it!" cried Jack. "I found the treasure chest!"

"Forget the treasure chest!" said Annie. "We have to go now! The storm's getting worse!"

Jack kept staring at the chest. Was there gold inside? Silver? Precious gems?

"Come on!" Now Annie was shouting from the tree house window.

But Jack couldn't tear himself away. He

brushed the rest of the muddy sand off the chest.

"Jack, forget the treasure chest!" cried Annie. "Let's go!"

"Go back!" squawked Polly.

Jack looked at the parrot. She was perched on the black rock.

He stared into her wise eyes. He thought he knew her—knew her from somewhere else.

"Go back, Jack," she said. She sounded like a person.

Okay. It was definitely time to go.

Jack took one last look at the treasure chest. He clutched the gold medallion. Then he took off, running toward the tree house.

His socks and rain boots were still there. He quickly pulled the boots on. He shoved the socks into his backpack.

The rope ladder was dancing wildly in the wind. Jack grabbed it.

The ladder swayed as Jack climbed. He was tossed this way and that. But he held on tight.

At last he pulled himself into the tree house.

"Let's go!" he cried.

Annie was already holding the Pennsylvania book. She pointed to the picture of Frog Creek.

"I wish we could go there!" she shouted.

The wind was already blowing hard. But now it blew even harder.

The tree house started to spin. It spun faster and faster.

Then everything was still.

Absolutely still.

9

The Mysterious M

Drip, drip.

Jack opened his eyes.

Rain was dripping from the leaves of the tree.

They were back in Frog Creek. The rain was softer. The wind was gentler. The air was sweeter.

"Oh man." Jack sighed. "That was close." He was still holding the gold medallion.

"Polly's gone," said Annie sadly. "I was hoping she might come back with us."

"No magic creature has ever come back with us," said Jack.

He pulled off his backpack. It was damp with rain and saltwater.

Jack took out the pirate book. He put it on the stack of books. On top of the dinosaur book. And the knight book. And the mummy book.

Then Jack put the gold medallion beside the bookmark with the letter M.

Next he went down onto his knees. And ran his finger over the shimmering M on the floor. "We didn't find any M's on this trip," he said.

"Or the M person," said Annie.

Squawk!

"Polly!" Annie cried.

The parrot swooshed into the tree house.

She perched on the stack of books.

Polly looked straight at Jack.

"What—what are you doing here?" he asked her.

Slowly Polly raised her bright green wings. They grew bigger and bigger until they spread out like a huge green cape.

Then, in a great swirl of colors—in a blur of feathers and light—in a flapping and stretching and screeching—a new being took shape.

Polly was not a parrot any longer. In her place was an old woman. A beautiful old woman with long white hair and piercing eyes.

She wore a green feathered cape. She perched on the stack of books. And she was very calm and very still.

Neither Jack nor Annie could speak. They were too amazed.

"Hello, Jack. Hello, Annie," the old woman said. "My name is Morgan le Fay."

10

Treasure Again

Annie found her voice first. "The M person," she whispered.

"Yes. I'm the M person," said Morgan.

"Wh-where are you from?" asked Jack.

"Have you ever heard of King Arthur?" said Morgan.

Jack nodded.

"Well, I am King Arthur's sister," said Morgan.

"You're from Camelot," said Jack. "I've read about Camelot."

"What did you read about me, Jack?" said Morgan.

"You—you're a witch."

Morgan smiled. "You can't believe *everything* you read, Jack."

"But are you a magician?" said Annie.

"Most call me an enchantress. But I'm also a librarian," said Morgan.

"A librarian?" said Annie.

"Yes. And I've come to the 20th century, your time, to collect books. You are lucky to be born in a time with so many books."

"For the Camelot library?" asked Jack.

"Precisely," said Morgan. "I travel in this tree house to collect words from many different places around the world. And from many different time periods."

"Did you find books here?" said Jack.

"Oh yes. Many wonderful books. I want to

borrow them for our scribes to copy."

"Did you put all the bookmarks in them?" said Jack.

"Yes. You see, I like the pictures in the books. Sometimes I want to visit the scenes in the pictures. So all the bookmarks mark places I wish to go."

"How do you get there?" asked Annie.

"I placed a spell on the tree house," said Morgan. "So when I point to a picture and make the wish, the tree house takes me there."

"I think you dropped this in dinosaur times," said Jack.

He handed the gold medallion to Morgan.

"Oh, thank you! I wondered where I'd lost it," she said. She put the medallion into a hidden pocket in her cape.

"So can anybody work the spell?" asked

Annie. "Anybody who tries it?"

"Oh dear, no! Not just anybody," Morgan said. "You two are the only ones besides me to do it. No one else has ever even seen my tree house before."

"Is it invisible?" asked Annie.

"Yes," said Morgan. "I had no idea it would ever be discovered. But then you two came along. Somehow you hooked right into my magic."

"H-how?" asked Jack.

"Well, for two reasons, I think," explained Morgan. "First, Annie believes in magic. So she actually saw the tree house. And her belief helped you to see it, Jack."

"Oh man," said Jack.

"Then you picked up a book, Jack. And because you love books so much, you caused my magic spell to work."

"Wow," said Annie.

"You can't imagine my dismay when you started to take off for dinosaur times. I had to make a very quick decision. And I decided to come along."

"Oh, so you were the pteranodon!" said Annie.

Morgan smiled.

"And the cat and the knight and Polly!" said Annie.

"Yes," said Morgan softly.

"You were all these things to help us?" asked Jack.

"Yes, but I must go home now. The people in Camelot need my help."

"You're leaving?" whispered Jack.

"I'm afraid I must," said Morgan.

She picked up Jack's backpack and handed it to him. Jack and Annie picked up their rain-

63

coats. It had stopped raining.

"You won't forget us, will you?" asked Annie, as they put their raincoats on.

"Never," said Morgan. She smiled at both of them. "You remind me too much of myself. You love the impossible, Annie. And you love knowledge, Jack. What better combination is there?"

Morgan le Fay touched Annie's forehead gently. And then Jack's. She smiled.

"Good-bye," she said.

"Good-bye," said Annie and Jack.

Annie left the tree house first. Jack followed. They climbed down the rope ladder for the last time.

They stood below the oak tree and looked up.

Morgan was looking out the window. Her long white hair blew in the breeze.

Suddenly the wind began to blow.

The leaves began to shake.

A loud whistling sound filled the air.

Jack covered his ears and squeezed his eyes shut.

Then everything was silent.

Absolutely silent.

Jack opened his eyes.

The tree house was gone.

All gone.

Absolutely gone.

Annie and Jack stood a moment, staring up at the empty oak tree. Listening to the silence.

Annie sighed. "Let's go," she said softly.

Jack just nodded. He felt too sad to speak. As they started walking, he put his hands into his pockets.

He felt something.

Jack pulled out the gold medallion. "Look!"

he said. "How did—?"

Annie smiled. "Morgan must have put it there," she said.

"But how?"

"Magic," said Annie. "I think it means she'll be coming back."

Jack smiled. He clutched the medallion as he and Annie took off through the wet, sunny woods.

As they walked, the sun shined through the woods. And all the wet leaves sparkled.

Everything, in fact, was shining.

Leaves, branches, puddles, bushes, grass, vines, wild flowers—all glittered like jewels.

Or gleamed like gold.

Annie had been right, thought Jack.

Forget the treasure chest.

They had treasure at home. A ton of it. Everywhere.

Don't miss
Magic Tree House® #5
NIGHT OF THE NINJAS

Jack and Annie learn
the secrets of the ninjas!

Available now!

Here's a special preview of
Magic Tree House® Fact Tracker
Pirates

After their adventure on the beach,
Jack and Annie wanted to know more about
pirates. Track the facts with them!

Available now!

Excerpt copyright © 2001 by Will Osborne and Mary Pope Osborne.
Illustrations copyright © 2001 by Sal Murdocca. Published by Random House
Children's Books, a division of Penguin Random House LLC, New York.

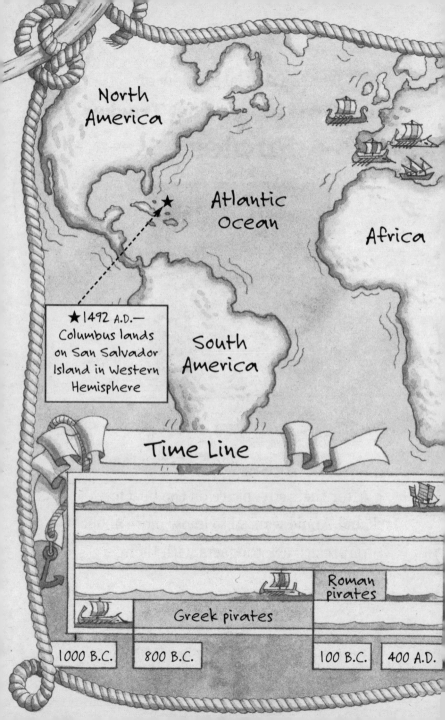

North
America

Atlantic
Ocean

Africa

★ 1492 A.D.—
Columbus lands
on San Salvador
Island in Western
Hemisphere

South
America

Time Line

Roman
pirates

Greek pirates

1000 B.C.   800 B.C.   100 B.C.   400 A.D.

Europe

Mediterranean Sea

Asia

Pacific Ocean

Indian Ocean

Australia

all dates are approximate

	Far East pirates			
		Barbary corsairs		
	Vikings			

| 700 A.D. | 1000 A.D. | | 1500 A.D. | 2000 A.D. |

How to Be a Buccaneer

Buccaneers were famous for their dirty, stinky ways. Here's how to become a buccaneer:

1. *Don't bathe or change clothes!*

Buccaneers didn't wash for months at a time. They made their clothes from animal skins and dressed in the same clothes every day—until they wore out!

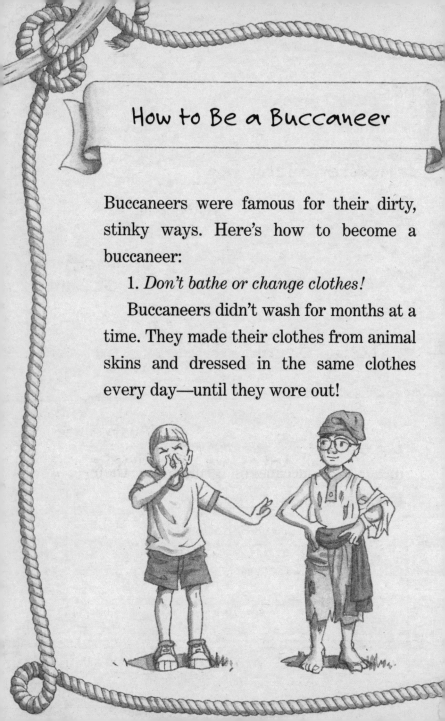

2. *Don't wear shoes!*

Buccaneers almost always went barefoot, even when they attacked a ship.

3. *Have a barbecue!*

Ships from all over the world stopped at the buccaneers' islands for hides, water, and supplies. The sailors often enjoyed the meat the buccaneers grilled on their boucans.

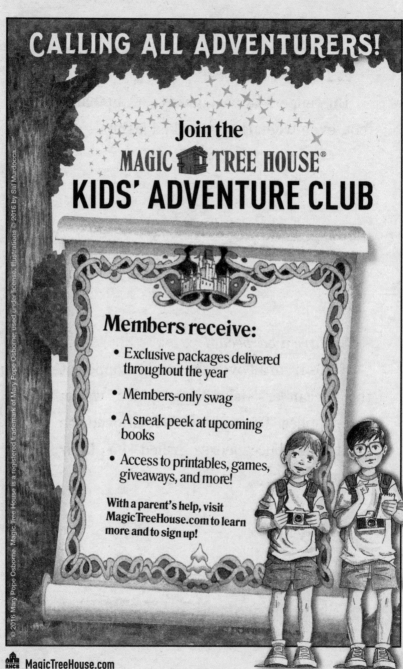